THE 1925 SERUM RUN

ANCHORAGE TO NENANA TO NOME

BY RAILROAD

BY DOGSLED

NENANA

ALASKA RANGE

ANCHORAGE

Robert J. Blake

PHILOMEL BOOKS

TOGO

eonhard Seppala shook his head.
He carefully watched every new
pup, hoping to see that special
one—a pup that would grow into the
perfect dog to lead his sled-racing team.

But it was unlikely to be this pup, the
one he called Togo. He was too small,
too independent and too wild for his
team.

So one day, when a woman came to
his kennel looking for a pet, Seppala
said, "I've got just the dog for you!"
And he gave her Togo.

But Togo didn't want to be a pet. He wanted to be a sled dog. He crashed through the woman's parlor window and ran all the way home to be with the team.

"Any dog that wants to be here that badly can stay!" was what Seppala said.

When Seppala's team wasn't racing, he and the dogs hauled freight all over Alaska. One stormy day, when Togo was only eight months old, Seppala planned to leave him behind while he took the team on an overnight supply run to a place called Dime Creek.

"Keep that pup behind the fence!" Seppala called to the kennel helper as he and his team pulled away.

But the fence did not stop Togo. Late that night he found a way to escape and chased after the team.

It was snowing hard the next morning on the trail, so Seppala harnessed the team and took off before dawn. By daylight the dogs had lost their way.

Suddenly, all ears went up. The team bolted forward as if the dogs had caught a scent.

Reindeer? Seppala wondered. A fox?

A dog stepped into view.

"Togo!" Seppala sighed. "You look like you ran all night!"

The next day Togo was allowed to run free around the team. He nipped and barked at the team. Seppala knew his dogs would never find the trail with Togo distracting them. He put the dog in harness at the back of the team just to keep him under control.

"That will slow you down," Seppala said. But it didn't. Togo easily kept the pace.

Surprised, Seppala moved Togo up to a position in the center of the line. When they took off, Togo pulled harder than any other dog.

"All right then," Seppala said, and moved Togo to the lead position. "Let's see if you can get us back on track."

Togo easily found the trail.

Although small for a Siberian husky, Togo was very strong. He had a perfect sense of direction and always tried to travel in a straight line. Right from the start he got the team where they needed to go, though he often plowed them through a snowbank to get there.

In 1918 Seppala entered Togo in his first race, the Borden Marathon. The next year they set the record for the fastest time ever in that event.

Race after race it was always the same—Togo's team the winners. Seppala became known as the fastest man in North America.

"It's because of that dog Togo," everybody said.

Then, one icy January day, there came a desperate knock on Seppala's door.

"Diphtheria," the man's voice cut through the freezing wind. "A young boy . . . it is so contagious that in two weeks it could wipe out everyone here in Nome!" He tried to catch his breath. "Anchorage has an antitoxin that can stop it, but the train from Anchorage only goes as far as Nenana."

Nenana was 600 miles from Nome!

"A dog team has volunteered to bring the serum from Nenana to Nulato." Still 300 miles away from Nome. "You have the fastest team in Alaska. Would you make the run to Nulato and bring back the serum?"

"When do you need it?" Seppala asked.

"Yesterday," said the man.

January 28, 1925

Newspaper headlines around the world shouted out the story:

NOME'S DEADLY RACE AGAINST TIME AND THE ELEMENTS

It usually took the U.S. mail system thirty days to make the run from Nenana to Nome. But now, in the middle of winter, the mushers didn't have thirty days. Nome had no more than two weeks before the diphtheria devastated the city.

Togo's eyes followed Seppala as he carefully chose the dogs for this run. Only the fastest, most trail-smart and obedient dogs would do. At last the team was set, with Togo in the lead.

Seppala called out to him with his familiar clucking sounds, *tlk, tlk,* and the team left Nome.

The team soon settled down behind Togo. The only sounds were the shush of the sled and the breathing of the dogs. With just six hours of daylight this time of year, Seppala set a quick pace and made the thirty miles into Solomon as the sun set.

January 29, 1925

On the second day a strong wind came up, drifting snow over the trail. Togo, with his good trail sense, carefully avoided stumps and holes and anything hidden under the snow. The going was slow.

Seppala decided to take a shortcut across frozen Golovin Bay. As soon as he and the dogs stepped onto the bay, the wind increased, blowing away the snow and leaving only hard, slick ice.

They made it into Golovin on schedule, but it was anyone's guess as to whether Togo led them or the wind blew them into the village that night.

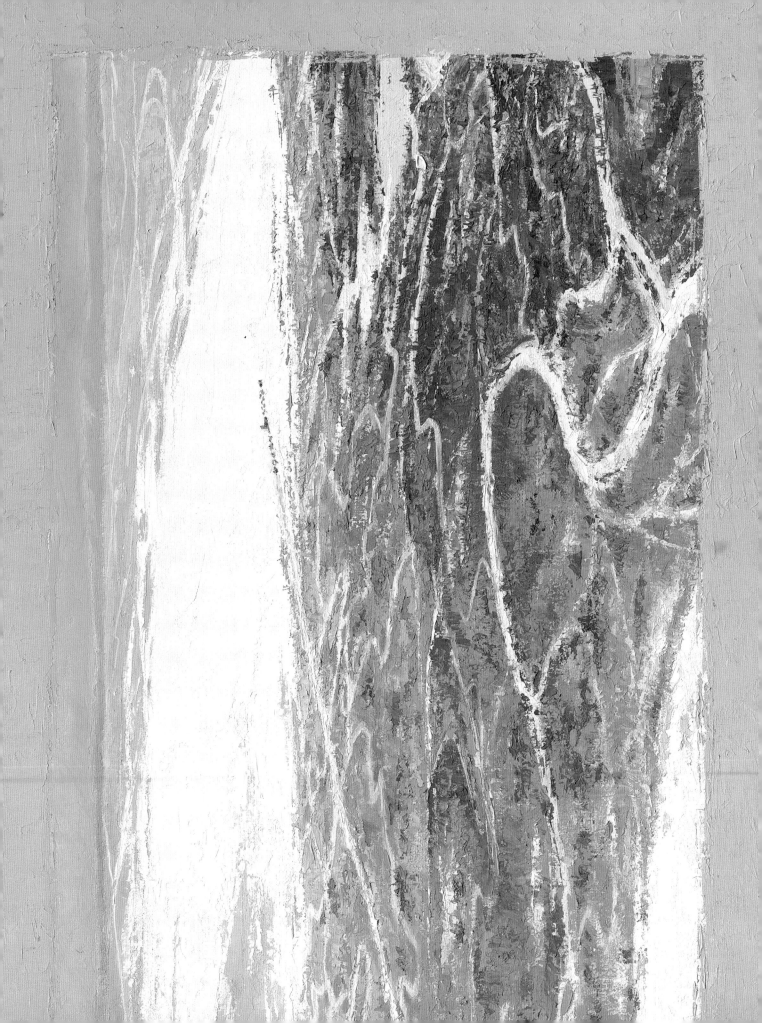

When they got to Golovin, the news was bad. "Things are getting worse in Nome. They've radioed to say that if the relay takes two weeks, the serum will arrive too late," his host told the musher. Seppala did not get much sleep that night.

January 30, 1925

Seppala set out early the next day and drove the team hard to cover the fifty-three miles to Isaac's Point. Maybe too hard.

"How're the dogs?" a man asked him.

"Holdin' up," the musher answered.

But as he looked over the team, he seemed concerned.

January 31, 1925

Seppala woke and sat straight up. Something was wrong. He cocked his ear and listened. Quickly, he jumped out of bed and looked out the window.

"The wind has changed," he said aloud. Togo was waiting for him outside.

"Wind's comin' straight in from the bay now. It'll break up the ice." Seppala quickly harnessed the team. "If we're going to make it across Norton Bay, we've got to do it now!

"Okay, Togo, lead 'em out!" he called.

Far out in front of the sled, Togo read the ice. He looked for cracks, felt for loose water and listened for any sound of ice breaking. The wind never let up.

Seppala shifted on the sled and put his hand to his back. He could feel it in his bones—the weather was changing, a storm was coming in. "Hup, hup," he called. "Faster!"

They had to get across Norton Bay before the weather pinned them down and the ice broke up.

Hour after hour they ran. The dog Smokey was struggling, the team needed a rest. Then Togo's ears went up. He shifted his gait and looked off to the side. There, just ahead, was another team, fighting among themselves.

Seppala called, *"Ssshk, ssshk, run through, run through!"*

Suddenly, words from the other team jumped off the wind. *"Serum! Turn back!"*

They had almost run right past the serum!

The other musher ran up to Seppala. "I was sent from Shaktoolik to intercept you. The epidemic in Nome has gotten worse!" he hollered over the wind.

"Teams have been added so that the serum can travel both day and night!"

Seppala breathed a sigh of relief and looked at his exhausted team. "I guess you will be taking the serum on to Nome, then."

The man looked back at his own team. "They've been fighting since we left the village. They won't make it," he said. "You've got the better team. You gotta turn back and deliver the serum to the next relay man. In Golovin."

Return to Golovin! Seppala squinted back through the storm building over the bay. Golovin was ninety miles back, and now they would have to cross Norton Bay again—this time head-on into the wind.

He looked down at his own team. It desperately needed rest. All the dogs were lying down.

Except one. Togo stood pawing the ice.

"Give me the serum," Seppala growled.

Seppala packed the serum and moved the team out. They hugged the land as long as they could. But finally, Seppala gave the command "Togo, haw!" and Togo turned left to move his team back onto the ice of Norton Bay.

Immediately the weather attacked the team. Togo fought the wind, struggling to keep the sled on course. Seppala's gloved hands were knotted around the sled handle. The temperature was 40 below zero.

He kept thinking about the team: Too slow and the dogs would stiffen up. Too fast and just breathing hard would scorch their lungs. Seppala pulled the hood of his parka down. Togo would have to be his eyes and ears.

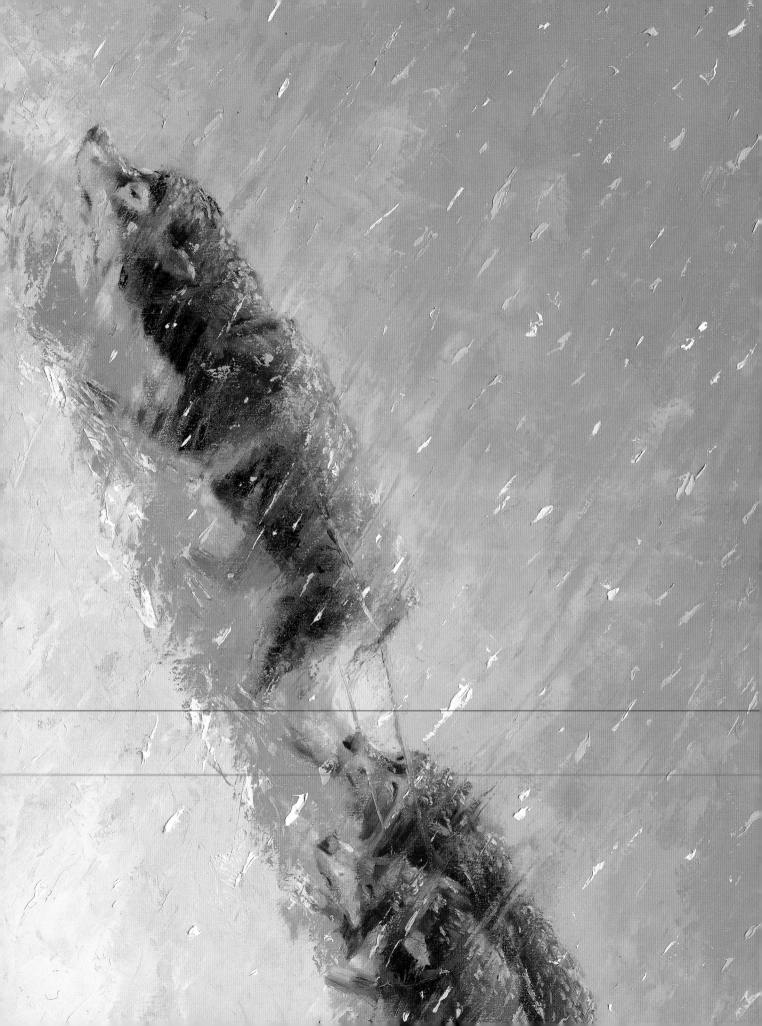

The snow drove into the dogs' faces like millions of tiny pins. They held their heads low and closed their eyes, allowing Togo to lead the way. Seppala was nodding off at the helm of the sled.

Seppala bolted awake. The team was slowing down. Their stomachs were beginning to freeze where their fur was thin. Seppala stopped the team and ran to his dogs. His fingers froze instantly when he threw off his gloves. He massaged each dog's stomach with his bare hands.

Quickly, he got the team under way again.

Inch by inch the team worked its way across the bay. Suddenly the wind kicked the sled on its side. The big dog Jens went down, a line twisted around his neck. Dogs scrambled in all directions, pulling the line taut. Seppala made a grab for the line and a dog made a lunge for his arm.

Togo barked. The dogs backed off. Seppala loosed Jens and untangled the lines. Then they were off again.

Hour after hour it was the same. Snow. Bitter cold. Wind.

The storm grew worse. Growls were heard, tempers were wearing thin. Seppala was concerned that if they did not find a place to warm the serum soon, it might freeze.

The weather doubled its fury. Seppala pushed the team harder, stopping only briefly at an igloo to warm the serum.

Out on the Norton Bay ice, the big dog Jens collapsed again and was dragged a quarter mile. The dog called Johnson's eyes froze shut. Seppala cleared them using his own breath. Then Smokey refused to run any farther. Even Togo could not get him to move.

The whole team came to a halt. Seppala jumped from the runners of the sled and grabbed Smokey by the collar.

"Get going, you . . ."

And then he felt Togo's eyes looking at him. Eyes that would not let go.

They said, *Your team has given you all they have.*

Seppala let Smokey out of harness. He twisted the lead line around his hands and looked over at Togo. "It's up to you and me. Let's bring this team in."

Time, events, places all ran together. Through the cold, through the storm, through the exhaustion, Togo and Seppala led the team.

Finally, late in the day, the dogs picked up a scent. Golovin Village. People. There was the other sled. The other team. Other musher.

Seppala handed over the serum. Another team would continue the relay to Nome.

EPILOGUE

Togo led his team over 350 miles on his part of the serum run. He gave so much of himself that he was never able to race again.

Another dog and another team would become famous for running only fifty-three miles of the serum run. That team was led by a kennel mate of Togo's, a dog named Balto. People honored Balto for being the lead dog of the team that finally brought the serum into Nome. And certainly, every dog that participated in the serum run is a hero. But to this day many people in Alaska have concerns about Togo's part in the run being ignored. They feel, as others have, that the hero is not always the dog who crosses the finish line first, but, as in this case, the dog who made the last lap even possible.

For many, the annual Iditarod Race commemorates the historic serum run of 1925, the race traveling through Shaktoolik, Golovin and many of the same villages as Leonhard Seppala and the other mushers did on their heroic mission.

AUTHOR'S NOTE

For this story I traveled to the villages that Togo went through for his part of the journey. While in Alaska I heard many different versions of the 1925 serum run to Nome. For example, I discovered discrepancies concerning the type of lead Togo was on and if he was at times allowed to run free of the line. I have shown him both on a lead and free.

Only Leonhard Seppala and Togo know exactly what went on with the team as they ran their part of the relay. This story is how I imagine it may have been, based on the information I gathered. More than anything, I have tried to re-create the feel of their struggle.

I would like to thank the many people who put me up and took the time to talk to me as I did my research in Nome, Solomon, Golovin, Koyuk, Elim, Unalakleet, Shaktoolik and Anchorage. Thanks Mary B., Mary K., Marty O., Tim H., and Lyn F.

I offer a very special thank you to my new friend and Togo aficionado, Barbara Narendra of the Yale Peabody Museum.

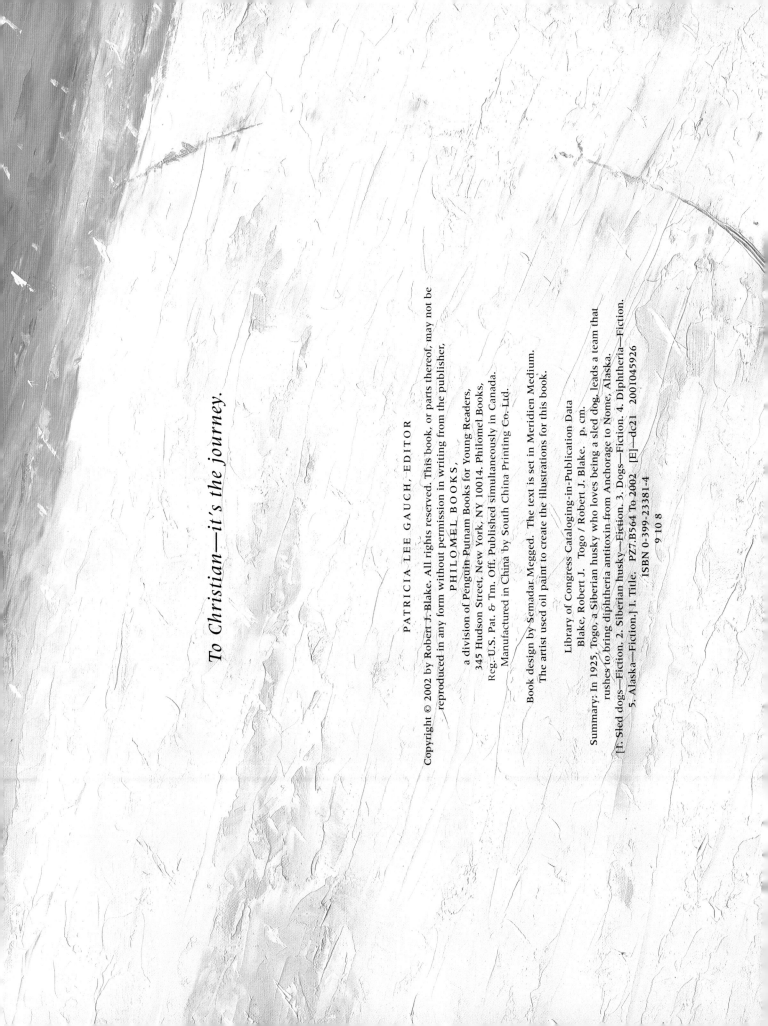

To Christian—it's the journey.

PATRICIA LEE GAUCH, EDITOR

PHILOMEL BOOKS,
a division of Penguin Putnam Books for Young Readers,
345 Hudson Street, New York, NY 10014. Philomel Books,
Reg. U.S. Pat. & Tm. Off. Published simultaneously in Canada.
Manufactured in China by South China Printing Co. Ltd.

Book design by Semadar Megged. The text is set in Meridien Medium.
The artist used oil paint to create the illustrations for this book.

Library of Congress Cataloging-in-Publication Data
Blake, Robert J. Togo / Robert J. Blake. p. cm.
Summary: In 1925, Togo, a Siberian husky who loves being a sled dog, leads a team that
rushes to bring diphtheria antitoxin from Anchorage to Nome, Alaska.
[1. Sled dogs—Fiction. 2. Siberian husky—Fiction. 3. Dogs—Fiction. 4. Diphtheria—Fiction.
5. Alaska—Fiction.] I. Title. PZ7.B564 To 2002 [E]—dc21 2001045926
ISBN 0-399-23381-4
9 10 8

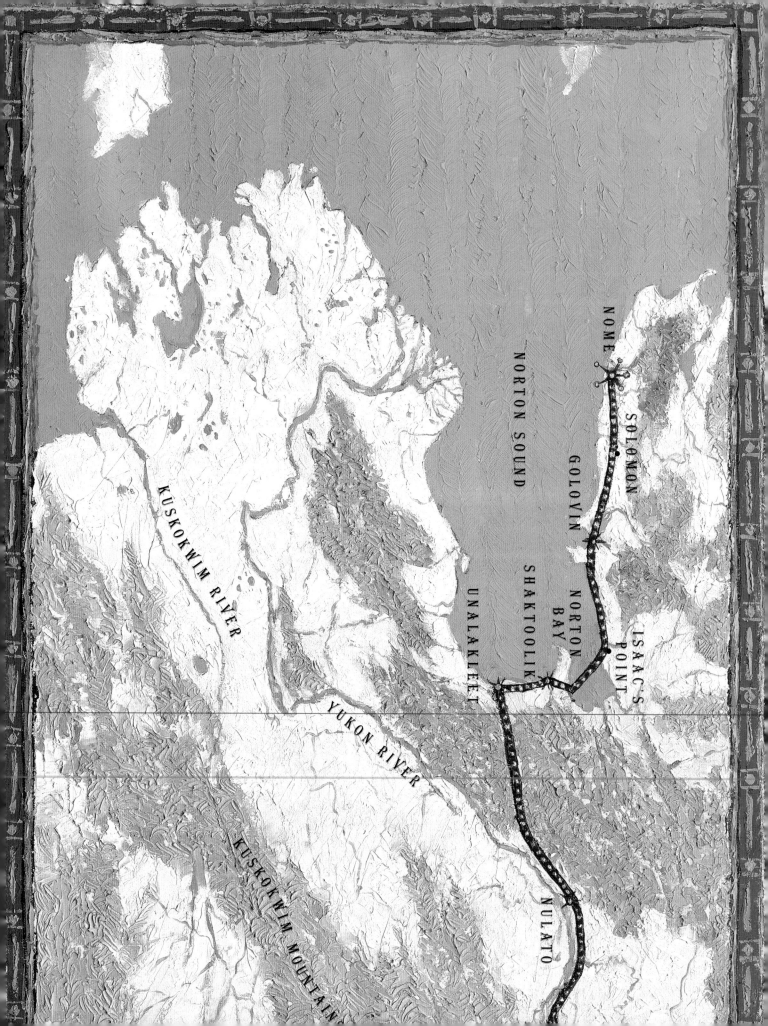

NOME

SOLOMON

NORTON SOUND

GOLOVIN

ISAAC'S POINT

NORTON BAY

SHAKTOOLIK

UNALAKLEET

KUSKOKWIM RIVER

YUKON RIVER

NULATO

KUSKOKWIM MOUNTAINS